THE THING IN THE BASEMENT

DANGER!
DO
NOT
ENTER!

by Michaela Morgan
illustrated by Doffy Weir

PICTURE WINDOW BOOKS
Minneapolis, Minnesota

Editor: Jill Kalz
Page Production: Brandie Shoemaker
Art Director: Nathan Gassman
Associate Managing Editor: Christianne Jones

First American edition published in 2007 by
Picture Window Books
5115 Excelsior Boulevard
Suite 232
Minneapolis, MN 55416
877-845-8392
www.picturewindowbooks.com

First published in 2006 by A&C Black Publishers Limited, 38 Soho Square,
London W1D 3HB, with the title THE THING IN THE BASEMENT.

Printed in the United States of America.

Library of Congress Cataloging-in-Publication Data
Morgan, Michaela.
The thing in the basement / by Michaela Morgan ; illustrated by Doffy Weir.
p. cm. — (Read-it! chapter books)
Summary: There are strange noises, too much heat, dust, and dirt, all coming
from the basement of his new school, and Scott is sure that there is a dragon
living down there.
ISBN-13: 978-1-4048-3133-9 (library binding)
ISBN-10: 1-4048-3133-9 (library binding)
[1. Schools—Fiction. 2. Imagination—Fiction. 3. Dragons—Fiction.]
I. Weir, Doffy, ill. II. Title.
PZ7.M8255Th 2006
[Fic]—dc22   2006027271

Table of Contents

Chapter One

"I'll go in by myself," Scott said to his mom. "I *want* to go in by myself!" He looked at the other kids going through the tall gates. "I just don't want all of them to think I'm a scaredy cat."

"If you're sure," said Mom.

Scott waved and smiled cheerfully as his mom drove away. Then he slowly turned around to look at his new school.

The playground was
nearly empty now. Scott
heard a bell and knew
he should run in quickly,
but his legs felt
weak and shaky.

Scott's new
school was tall—very
tall. It was dark—very dark.
Everything about it was very strange,
very different, and very, very BIG!

All around the school there were high railings. It looked like a cage made to keep in some huge beast.

Scott could see two grimy, basement-level windows. The windows had bars across them.

"Was something being kept down there?" he wondered.

At his old house, Scott had gone to the school on the corner of his street. His old school was a small school. It had grass and trees all around it, and Scott had been happy there. He had lots of really good friends.

He didn't know anybody at this new place. Not one single person.

Scott took a deep breath, went through the gates, and across the playground. All he could hear was the sound of his own footsteps. He felt a little sick.

Scott pushed open the door into the school and stepped inside. It was quiet—very quiet. He peered into the office.

The secretary was busy talking on the phone. She didn't see him. In the distance, he could hear strange music and chanting.

"They've already started class. That's why it's so quiet," he told himself, but he couldn't stop shaking.

Would he get in trouble for being late?

Late on his very first day!

"I'll just go right to my classroom. I'm sure I can remember the way," Scott told himself.

The principal had showed Scott and his mom all around the school only a week ago.

Scott headed down the hallway. Five minutes later, he was lost.

There were so many hallways! So many stairs! He was now in a dark hallway. It was long and empty. It looked deserted, and it smelled dusty and strange.

Scott had not seen this part of the school on his visit. Was this part of the school kept a secret?

Slowly, he walked to the very end of the hallway. There, tucked into the corner, were some concrete stairs. These stairs led downward.

Scott peered down the dark stairs. There were big, black footprints leading to a closed door. On the door was a sign:

DANGER! DO NOT ENTER!

Chapter Two

It was then that Scott noticed the smell. It was a smell of heat, dust, and burning. It was a very strange smell, and it was coming from behind the door at the bottom of the stairs.

"What could be down there?"
Scott wondered.

He could feel heat rising.
He could see light coming
through the cracks around
the door. Suddenly there
was a flash and a roar.

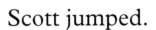

Scott jumped.

There was something in the
basement! And it was something
nasty ... something monstrous.

"What should I do? What should I do?" he worried.

And then there was another

FLASH! and a

and a BANG!

RRRRrrrroar!

Scott didn't stop to think. He ran.

He ran and ran and ran.
Up stairs ...

... along hallways ...

... and around
corners.

His heart was thumping hard in
his chest. He scrambled around
another corner, and then he saw
where he was.

He was outside his classroom. He knew it by the name on the door and the display of dragon paintings on the walls.

Mrs. Archer, his new teacher, had pointed it out last week when he was visiting the school.

"We all did a fantastic project on dragons," she had said. "Everybody in this school is a dragon expert!"

Suddenly Scott knew the truth. There really was something in the basement. And that "something" was a dragon.

There was a dragon coiled up and breathing fire below his new school!

Chapter Three

Scott crept into the classroom.

"Sorry I'm late," he muttered.
But Mrs. Archer was busy,
opening windows. She just
waved at him to sit down at
the front table.

"Don't worry. I'll deal with you in a minute," she said.

There was a red-haired boy and two girls at Scott's table. The boy smiled and whispered his name.

"I'm Damon," he said.

The two girls just nodded and continued with their work.

The classroom was very quiet. The only sound was a strange, distant gurgling and glugging. And it was so *hot*.

Everyone had taken off their sweaters. Some kids were trying to fan themselves with notebooks, but no one was complaining.

It was so hot that Scott could hardly breathe. He looked around.

"Why wasn't anybody saying anything?" he wondered. "Why was everybody acting as though it was completely normal to be boiled alive in a classroom? And what was that odd noise?"

The gurgling and glugging seemed to be getting louder and louder. And closer and closer?

Scott couldn't stand it any longer. He had a terrible feeling that something awful was going to happen. Shyly, he put up his hand.

"Please, Mrs. Archer," he said. "It's boiling hot ... and there's a very strange noise ..."

"Oh that!" said Mrs. Archer. "It's just Stovie up to his tricks again. We'll have to get Mr. Crawley to sort it out. He's the only one who can control the beast."

"Should I go down to the basement and find him?" asked Damon.

"NO!" snapped the teacher. "I've told you before. No one is to go to the basement—EVER. It's very dangerous. Is that clear?"

Everyone nodded.
Someone sighed. Mrs. Archer
opened another window.

And then a strange
man came into
the room. The
man was
enormously tall
and very, very
hairy. He had
a thick beard,
long, red hair,
and bushy
eyebrows. He
was the hairiest
man Scott had
ever seen.

There was even
hair sprouting out of
his ears and nose!

But the strangest
thing was that he
was covered in
black streaks and
soot. His hands
and fingernails
were dirty, and a
nasty, burning smell
surrounded him.

"Is that the
dragon keeper?"
Scott wondered.

"Who's that?" whispered Scott.

"It's Creepy Crawley!" said Damon. "He's the one who looks after Stovie. Don't get on the wrong side of him!"

Mr. Crawley spoke to Mrs. Archer. "I'm sorry," he said. "The beast isn't behaving today. I may have overfed it. We're all going to roast!"

Soon it was playtime. Scott didn't like the idea of going into the playground with a lot of children he had never met before. And he couldn't stop thinking about the thing in the basement. It was all so strange that he was beginning to think he had imagined it.

He took a deep breath and decided he would try to find those steps. He would try to find the dragon.

Chapter Four

Scott went to find the basement steps again. It wasn't easy, and he was worried that he would meet a teacher and have to explain where he was going. He didn't want to have to explain. He didn't want to get into trouble. He was just about to give up—then he saw the steps.

"Don't be scared," he said to himself. "Just go up to the door, and peep through the crack."

Scott followed the trail of sooty marks ... down one stair ... then two ... then three.

He tried not to be scared of the smells. He tried not to be scared by the gurgling and glugging sounds coming through the door. He tried not to be scared of the shadows. But then he heard the sound of footsteps, and the door at the bottom of the stairs opened ...

It was the hairy
man. Creepy Crawley.
The dragon keeper!

DANGER!
DO
NOT
ENTER

"What are you doing down here?" roared Mr. Crawley. "No children are allowed here! I'm taking you straight to the principal's office!"

And that's what he did.

Soon Scott was standing in front of Mrs. Witchley, the principal.

"What's all this about?" Mrs. Witchley asked.

"I ... I ... was trying to see the thing in the basement," Scott stuttered. "I've heard it roaring. I've felt its heat. I know you've got a dragon down there!"

Mrs. Witchley shook her head. "He knows you're keeping a dragon, Mr. Crawley," she sighed. Then she looked at Scott and said, "I think it's time we introduced you to Stovie. Take him down to the basement, Mr. Crawley!"

As they marched back down the maze of long, dark corridors, Scott's mind was bubbling with thoughts and fears.

Why are they taking me back to the basement?

What are they going to do?

Are they going to feed me to the **dragon?**

At the bottom of the concrete steps, Mr. Crawley swung the door open. Mrs. Witchley stood back. There was a terrible wave of heat and sound.

"Scott, meet Stovie. Stovie, this is Scott," said Mr. Crawley.

Scott had never seen anything like it. It was huge, noisy, and covered in the blackest soot.

But it wasn't a dragon.

Chapter Five

"Stovie is our old boiler," Mrs. Witchley explained. "It heats the school. That's *heats*, not *eats*, the school! Sometimes it makes it a bit too hot—like today," she smiled.

"Oh," Scott said, his voice sounding very small. He knew his face was turning red—and it wasn't just because of the heat.

"Only Mr. Crawley knows how to control the old thing," explained Mrs. Witchley. "We always say Stovie's a bit of a beast—but I never thought of calling it a dragon!"

40

Scott felt small and silly.
His face was now bright red—
except for the places where it
was streaked with soot. He came
up the basement stairs slowly,
one step at a time. Behind him
came Mrs. Witchley and
Mr. Crawley.

Mrs. Witchley brushed soot and cobwebs from her hair. "We don't allow children to come down here. The place is too hot and dirty. It just isn't safe."

Scott kept his eyes fixed on his feet. He had never felt so silly in all his life.

There was no dragon.

There was no mystery.

There was just a big, dark school where he didn't have any friends. He sighed. Life couldn't get any worse. Then he looked up.

Damon and the two girls from his table were coming down the hallway, and they were pointing at him.

"Oh, no!" thought Scott. "Now everyone is going to make fun of me."

"There you are!" said Damon. "We've been looking everywhere for you. Do you want to play with us?"

"You're all covered in soot!" said one of the girls. "What happened?"

So Scott told them.

"What an adventure!" said Damon. "I wish I could solve a mystery like you did."

Scott smiled. He was feeling much

 better now. He had some new friends. No one was making fun of him—and he wasn't afraid of a dragon anymore.

They all went out into the playground, and Scott pointed at the basement windows. "I can't believe I thought there was a dragon living down there!" he laughed.

It was then that they heard the growl—a long, deep growl. The new friends looked at each other. Perhaps there *was* a thing in the basement, after all! Maybe they could solve the mystery together.

Look for More *Read-it!* Chapter Books

The Badcat Gang
Beastly Basil
Cat Baby
Cleaner Genie
Clever Monkeys
Contest Crazy
Disgusting Denzil
Duperball
Elvis the Squirrel
Eric's Talking Ears
High Five Hank
Hot Dog and the Talent Competition
Nelly the Monstersitter
On the Ghost Trail
Scratch and Sniff
Sid and Bolter
Stan the Dog Becomes Superdog
Tough Ronald

Looking for a specific title? A complete list
of *Read-it!* Chapter Books is available on our Web site:
www.picturewindowbooks.com